TAKE FIVE

Margaret G. Arnold

ARTHUR H. STOCKWELL LTD
Torrs Park, Ilfracombe, Devon, EX34 8BA
Established 1898
www.ahstockwell.co.uk

© Margaret G. Arnold, 2021
First published in Great Britain, 2021

The moral rights of the author have been asserted

All rights reserved.
No part of this publication may be reproduced
or transmitted in any form or by any means,
electronic or mechanical, including photocopy,
recording, or any information storage and
retrieval system, without permission
in writing from the copyright holder.

British Library Cataloguing-in-Publication Data.
A catalogue record for this book is available
from the British Library.

This is an entirely fictional story,
and no conscious attempt has been made
to accurately record or recreate
any real-life events.

ISBN 978-0-7223-5063-8
Printed in Great Britain by
Arthur H. Stockwell Ltd
Torrs Park   Ilfracombe
Devon

THANK YOU!

I am grateful to the group of talented and gifted published authors known as Bewdley Bards, who have so generously encouraged and inspired me to write. My thanks go especially to, in alphabetical order, Heather Flack, Rita Hardiman, Pauline Rice and Tony Smith.

I would also like to thank the following;

Rose Nicholas of A. H. Stockwell Ltd for her kind assistance and guidance in publishing my book to its best advantage.

Judy Greenway, Acting Trustee for the Wilfrid Gibson Literary Estate who has generously allowed me to quote from Gibson's poem, "The Ice Cart".

My nephew Stephen Russell Mendham for his generosity in giving me permission to use some of his stunning photographs.

I am also very grateful to my husband Phillip for his patience while I have been compiling my book.

Margaret G. Arnold,
January 2020

CONTENTS

PART ONE – BEING HUMAN

No Inhibitions	9
A Family in Attendance	11
Game of Arches	13
I Can't Remember	15
I Did Not Know That	16
An Heroic Operation	18
The Deadly Chair	20
Science Fiction	22
A Revelation?	24
The Record Player	25
Beginning on the Major Road Ahead	28
The Shopping List	29
Punctuality	32
Drop In and Drop Out	34
A House Called Whispering Trees	37
Jealousy: Fine Feathers Make Fine Birds	39
The Attic Room	41
The Unveiling	44
These Figures Don't Stack Up	46
Postscript	49
Wandering	51
Waxing Lyrical	53
A Wild Night in Mallorca	55
The Piano	57
Suspense	59
No Desire Path	61
The Tray	62
Silence	64
The Penitent	65
The Spark Plugs of Inspiration	66
Profound Mother-Love	68
My Wonderful Mother, My Best Friend	70
Just Once Together	72
Impatience	73

PART TWO – PLANET EARTH

Truth Unsubdued	77
Helios, the God of the Sun	78
Modern Sun Worship	79
Birdsong	80
Kaleidoscope	81
Everything Held Dear	82
England in May	86
The Wonderful Winter Month of January	88
Out and About in the Wilds	90
Return of the Pine Marten, Return of the Scottish Wildcat	92
Wildcat	93
Earth Replies to the Sun	95
The Needy Lotos-eater	96
Alter Ego – A Dream	98
Keeping Within the Lines	100

PART THREE – VERSE AND WORSE

Quasimodo's Song	105
He Stole My Heart	106
Bodyguard	107
Impulse and Consequence	108
Mystique	109
How Is It . . . ?	110
Jingles the Troubadour	111

Part One

Being Human

NO INHIBITIONS

Oh, oh, my head! Thump! Thump! Who is in charge of this roundabout? It's turning much too fast – it's dangerous! I seem to be the only one on it. Oh, that's better – it's slowing down.

Where am I? This is not my bedroom. I must be in a hotel. I can't say I like the décor much! It's very unimaginative! White walls, white floor, white ceiling! There's no window that I can see, nor a door! And I can't see any furniture either.

It's very kind of the chambermaids – they've given me some nightclothes. Although the material is a bit tough, white like the room, and very tight, very restrictive. I need to wipe my nose, but my arms are pinned down. I must complain to the manager.

Who am I? I can't seem to think straight. The Judge accused me of being Violet Druggie, but I don't recognise the name. Uh ho, it's coming back to me gradually. Who was this Judge, and what right did *he* have to judge *me*? *I*'ve done nothing wrong. What about the mote in his own eye!

"You were discovered at two o'clock this morning," said the Judge, "on Hartlebury Common hacking away at the gorse with a machete. . . ."

Aha, that's a point: what has happened to my machete? I can't see it anywhere.

"You were shrieking obscenities. Why were you in possession of a machete?"

"I had to hack my way through the jungle, and I had to shriek to frighten the leopards, the snakes and the orang-utans."

"There are no leopards, snakes or orang-utans on Hartlebury Common."

"I was in the jungle. I had been harmlessly enjoying a celebration of Midsummer Night with some friends. Wayne had brought honey mead, Sharleen had brought champagne, and Crispin had brought strawberries covered in brandy cream. We passed a joint round, but I can't remember who brought that. It's all a bit hazy. When the party finished, my friends left me on my own and I got lost. That was when I accidentally wandered into the jungle."

The judge was not amused.

"You apparently have no inhibitions at all. When you were found you were wearing nothing but a daisy chain on your head."

That's another point: what had they done with my daisy chain? It had taken such a long time to plait it together. I was rather proud of my artistry.

The Judge continued his accusations against me: "Why did you think it necessary to take a machete with you to a celebration of Midsummer Night? Are you not aware it is an offence to carry a dangerous weapon?"

"I was a female alone in the dark. I needed to protect myself against any possible attacker."

The Judge gave me a piercing look. "You were completely without inhibitions – an affront to human dignity."

Well, I suppose I wasn't a very pretty picture. I'm seventy-nine, and can't be expected to look like a twenty-year-old. I am a bit wibbly-wobbly and droopy, but why blame me for that? God was the One with the drawing board and the assembly team.

The Judge was shaking his head sadly. "You are obviously not fit to plead. I am sending you to a secure mental unit for an indefinite period."

The next thing I knew was when I woke up in this unimaginative hotel room trussed up in these ill-designed nightclothes, like a turkey ready for the oven. I'm a bit annoyed about not having my machete – it was quite expensive. And that daisy chain was very pretty, but I shall have to make the best of it. Life can be a bit bothersome sometimes.

A FAMILY IN ATTENDANCE

Father had sent Mother to the clinic in Switzerland when I was three months old. He had hoped that the specialist care she would receive there, combined with the fresh, pure mountain air would improve her failing health. Today she was coming home again after a longer period of absence and recuperation than had been anticipated, and the whole family was in attendance.

Our family had been cared for by our two grandmothers and our mother's two elder sisters. On this memorable and edgy day they were keeping themselves busy, occasionally sending concerned glances in our direction.

The tea table was decorated with expensive linen bought specially for the occasion and completed with the family's best china and lead crystal. Everything was just as Mother would expect to find it – neat, clean and shiny.

Father was palely pacing the carpet, shoulders hunched. He had instructed my two brothers, my sister and myself to hold hands and stand with our backs to the fireplace, facing the door, when Mother arrived, and to stay still and quiet. There was an absence of coals in the grate as it was a hot afternoon in August. The heavy velvet curtains had been closed against the persistent sunshine in order to protect the colours in the carpet. The house was oppressively airless and still.

On that hot afternoon Mother arrived with red roses. Father had explained to us that they were Mother's favourite flowers. They symbolised love. I was eager to see her. How could I have known at the age of three months what she was like. When for the first time in my life I knowingly set eyes on her as she was brought in, she looked so small and delicate dressed in an emerald-green satin dress with satin shoes to match. Her auburn curls were arranged prettily around her dainty little face. She looked so fragile, like my broken porcelain doll.

The soberly dressed young men who had brought her into the room placed the white silk-lined open coffin in which she was lying in its designated place in the wide, shaded bay window. I sobbed uncontrollably.

GAME OF ARCHES

Seduced by the scent of the pine trees, I followed a footpath through the thick daylight-deprived forest until at last I found myself beyond the last trees. Stepping free of the undergrowth, I was dazzled by the suddenness of the bright sun. As my sight cleared, I was dazzled again by the sight of an immense arch made from glinting honey-coloured stone rising from a grassy plain. The arch divided a windowless wall of the same glinting material – a wall so tall it was impossible to see what lay beyond it. Harboured inside the arch was a stout wooden door. A large, black, heavy-looking wrought-iron key protruded from the keyhole.

At that time I was indulging myself in a solitary restorative walking holiday in Stirling in Scotland. Having lighted so suddenly and unexpectedly upon this immense and intriguing construction, I decided it was an excellent spot to have my lunch. Unfolding my picnic rug, I spread it on the grass and spread myself and my lunch on the rug. My lunch was a substantial meal prepared by my overnight bed-and-breakfast hostess which included a large slab of irresistible cake. Had I been Alice in Wonderland, the cake would have borne the unnecessary message, 'EAT ME', whereupon I would have immediately grown tall enough to see over the walls of this mysterious building.

The cake failed.

As I consumed the rest of my meal, having eaten the sweetmeat first, I began to imagine what the purpose of this wall and its arch might be. My first thought was the 1956 popular song warbled with gusto by Frankie Vaughan, 'Green Door': "There's an old piano and they play it hot behind the green door. Don't know what they're doing but they laugh a lot behind the green door." Well, this door was not green, and I couldn't hear an old piano being thumped.

I next considered the children's book by C. S. Lewis, *The Lion, the Witch and the Wardrobe*. Was there a magical land behind this provocative door, where a lion called Aslan was the king and god of Narnia? Was there a Wicked White Witch waiting to vent her evil upon whoever dared to open that stout wooden door? Since I was alone and unarmed, I hoped not.

Curiosity killed the cat, but I was not a cat, and my curiosity would not let me keep still. That mighty, black wrought-iron key with the elaborate pattern punched into its bow and shank turned easily in my hand, and I gave the door a push. Oh! Not what I had imagined!

Those overwhelming walls encompassed an overgrown patch of grass with faint hints that a honey-coloured floor had once been laid there. There was nothing else. Oh! Just a minute! What was that shiny object over there? I picked it up and turned it over. It was a silver platter engraved with words in an unrecognisable language. Had it been left behind unintentionally by an alien spacecraft? Had it once belonged to a Celtic princess, and could it therefore be designated treasure trove? Was it a recipe for a spell used by the Wizard Merlin on holiday from Wales? Was it an ancient recipe instead for haggis?

Still turning this beautiful object over in my fingers, I suddenly remembered that some scenes from the television programme *Game of Thrones*, with its own unique invented language, had been filmed in Stirling.

Could this wonderful, apparently ancient arch and wall once have been a part of the scenery designed for that programme?

I did not want it to be so. It was too extraordinary, too evocative, too beautiful to be abandoned as surplus to requirements and, sadly, only a sham.

The game I had played with my imagination while consuming my lunch began to fade with the sunlight. I folded my picnic rug into my backpack and continued with my walk.

I CAN'T REMEMBER

When I tell you I can't remember,
I know all too well it's a lie.
How can I forget what fell from your lips
Under the darkening sky.

And if I tell you I can't remember
The words that wounded me so,
The memory rises again in my soul
And I know that I can't let it go.

Must I say I can't remember the night,
Or the threat of rain, or even the place
Where the moonlight, cleaving the shadows,
Revealed my fate, clear in your face.

How could I say that I won't recall,
As the pitiless years roll by,
Our parting that night in the garden
When my heart could not understand why?

I DID NOT KNOW THAT

As a small child, my imagination was perpetually in motion. I had been born into a realm of startling sensations, and I considered it my duty to plunder that realm.

The Breeze curling through my fingers was a living creature. I had no right to seize it or deprive it of its freedom. When it touched my face, did it leave a mark, a trace of its own personality? Where had it come from? Where did it go?

When Time passed, was it like the Breeze? Did it have a presence? Could I feel it?

What was the nature of a Colour? Did it have a personality? I was told that Grass was Green. Was everything else that was smooth, cool and refreshing also Green? I was told that the Sky was Blue. What was the Sky? What did it mean? Could I touch it as I could the Grass? When I reached out to find the Sky, I was conscious of grasping only empty air. Was all empty air therefore Blue? Did a Colour possess a Perfume? Did it possess a Flavour? If I could not hear, feel, taste or smell a Colour, what was its purpose? Did everything have a Colour? Was Colour necessary for Life?

The voice of my mother's violin filled the room and filled my ears, but when I touched my ears searching for the Sound I could feel only my own flesh. What was the essence of Sound? Sound had Life, but no Body. How could I understand a Musical Note? It was something so transient, so elusive. Why could I not catch a Musical Note, hold it, weigh it, and, by turning it over in my hand, discover its shape?

Saying goodbye to a daytime of such adventures and discoveries is always disappointing for any small child, but my mother's warm, comforting tones as she read me a bedtime story always left me feeling safe and cherished, and soon asleep. Then, there was Tomorrow

– Tomorrow with all its fresh, startling sensations and endless questioning! It could not come soon enough! How I loved Tomorrow! Once again, there would be things to touch and feel, taste, hear and smell in the wonderful world that was waiting for me.

I was born blind.

But, as a small child, I did not know that.

AN HEROIC OPERATION
Fiction based on a real tragedy

In the small hours of that tragic September morning, the moon and stars had been vanquished and held imprisoned in a suffusing blackness. The louring sky was pierced from side to side with unrelenting cracks of lightning. The roaring of the waves crashing against the rocky outcrops of the Farne Islands echoed the thunder reverberating above.

Longstone Lighthouse was sending out its warning beams, but their feeble light held no protection against the gale-tossed, heavy open seas.

Troubled by the sounds of the storm, the daughter of the lighthouse keeper, whose bedroom was at the very top of the building, looked out and to her consternation discovered that a paddle steamer had foundered on the rocks of a neighbouring island. The combination of the fierce winds and the currents of the heaving seas had swung the vessel around, breaking it in two, and the part that had been left anchored perilously to the rocks was in danger of sinking.

Captain Hudson had taken his paddle steamer, the *Forfarshire*, heading north on a course for Dundee from Hull, on 5 September 1838 with sixty-one passengers, his crew and a cargo of cotton on board. During the voyage the weather had begun to worsen. The vessel's boilers failed, leaving her without power, abandoning her to the might of the storm. In desperation, the Captain had tried to find shelter for his vessel among the Farne Islands, but their treacherous rocks ensnared her as she was tossed helplessly on the waves and battered by the gales and relentless, steely rain.

Grace Darling, appalled at the tragedy confronting her, roused her father, William, with her urgent cries. Realising that it was too dangerous for the Seahouses lifeboat to set out, and that the distance was too great for its crew to offer immediate assistance, she and her father took out their rowing boat, their only available craft, trusting themselves to the mercy of God as they strove across the heaving sea, pounded by the gales and blinded by the driving rain. These two courageous souls had no concept of failure in their urgent mission.

The least dangerous route that could be followed by a rowing boat in these overwhelming conditions was more than a mile. As Grace and William approached the stricken paddle steamer, the cries of the few remaining survivors became mingled eerily with the screaming wind. Grace struggled with all her might to hold the rowing boat steady as the waves threatened to swamp it and crash it against the rocks. William discovered only nine survivors from the sixty-one passengers and crew. He drew on every ounce of strength he possessed as he hauled them from the constantly pitching-and-tossing wreckage to the rocking rowing boat while his valiant daughter fought to keep it steady.

After many hours of persistent and courageous battle against the gale-driven rain, the dazzling lightning and the raging seas, the rowing boat gained the safety of the lighthouse, where the elements continued to assail its stout walls for a further three days.

The selfless and courageous young woman, Grace Darling, was rewarded in many ways for her instant reaction to the tragic wrecking of the *Forfarshire* paddle steamer. Poets and artists ensured her enduring memory; Queen Victoria added her praises; the Royal National Institution for the Preservation of Life from Shipwreck presented her with a Silver Medal for Bravery. Financial rewards and many proposals of marriage were poured upon her, but she chose to remain modestly and quietly in her beloved home of Longstone Lighthouse with her mother and father.

THE DEADLY CHAIR
Fiction based on reality

Alfred Porter Southwick was born in 1826 in Buffalo, America. He was a slightly built man with an angelic face, blue eyes, blond hair, a seraphic smile and a gentle, retiring nature. He and his wife, an Irish immigrant called Mary Flynn, unable to have children of their own, had adopted a daughter. Alfred supported his happy little family by means of his own dental practice.

A nicer and more honest man you could not wish to meet. Respected and admired in his neighbourhood, he is reputed never to have harmed a fly.

However, behind his seraphic smile Alfred was nurturing a dark idea. In a dilapidated shed that was gradually disappearing under the murky and sinister greenery of an uncultivated corner of the generously sized garden, a deadly project was evolving. Neither Alfred's wife nor his daughter, and not even his cat, would venture there. Whatever he was doing under cover of darkness in his shed no one dared to ask. The flickering candlelight passing inside the dirty window was deliberately ignored. Its purpose was best left unknown. If Alfred's wife, Mary, did sometimes say to the nearby shopkeeper that she had no idea what Alfred was so involved with in his garden shed, it was generally agreed that the local dentist was a kind, humane, generous man, this fact being all it was necessary to know about him. Nevertheless, in some quarters there were evil rumours and unfriendly gossip.

After spending long nights working in his dilapidated shed, Alfred finally decided his project was nearing completion and needed to be moved to a workshop better suited for its finishing touches and eventual purpose.

Taking into account the mystery and the uninformed horrific rumours that had been spread, possibly by the shopkeeper, about the mysterious goings-on in the dentist's dilapidated shed, the jostling onlookers gathering outside the house were dumbstruck and deflated when they witnessed the removal of the mysterious project.

It turned out to be nothing more than a wooden chair, in a plain design that would not have disgraced a Quaker family. But it had holes where no hole had a right to exist, and a strange sort of headrest on the straight back implying that something else would be placed there. And there were leather straps attached to the arms and front legs.

It seemed that the nearest suitable workshop was in the local jail. The jostling onlookers, even more mystified than ever, shook their heads sadly and dispersed at the heavily guarded outer gates.

Housed inside the jail was a prisoner called William Kemmler, an alcoholic vegetable pedlar who had been sentenced to death for killing his common-law wife with a hatchet. His execution had been arranged for 6 August 1890. At just after six thirty that morning, his warder led him into the execution room.

The condemned man was somewhat bemused. He certainly had not expected to see such a contraption as the chair he was asked to occupy. And why should he be asked to try this novelty? Was he some sort of guinea pig? He calmly allowed himself to be strapped to the chair, and submitted his newly shaven head to the strange helmet poised on the headrest.

The grim purpose of the plain-looking chair with its attached leads soon became obvious.

William Kemmler smiled, and, resigned to his fate, said, "Gentlemen, I wish you all good luck!"

It took two shocks and seventeen minutes to send William Kemmler to his second and final judgment.

Alfred Porter Southwick, take a good look at your angelic face in the mirror – your blue eyes, your blond hair and your seraphic smile. Remember, you are reputed never to have harmed a fly. Despite your humane, generous nature and your belief that your deadly project was more merciful than a hangman's noose or a guillotine, can you honestly say to your reflection that you are not also a murderer?

SCIENCE FICTION

What country is this? Where am I? The ground beneath my feet is solid and black. There is no soil, although I see rows of trees. Where are the birds, the butterflies, the fields of poppies?

Are these people around me aliens? Are there no women in this city? These apparent aliens all wear identical uniforms, except for the differing colours. Are they poverty-stricken? They are all wearing trousers of a coarse blue material, ragged at the knees, topped with shapeless, baggy, grey or black jackets with hoods. Their feet are covered in heavy, clumsy boots. Surely I stand out as a foreigner in my long ecru linen tunic and my flimsy sandals, but no one looks at me. They all seem to be locked inside their own little world.

There seems to be a complete dependence on boxes! The buildings are composed of boxes of stone and steel piled one on top of another. Babies are confined to boxes on wheels. Their cries and frantic gesticulations go unnoticed, while the creatures guiding their boxes appear to be talking noisily to themselves with yet another small box clutched between one hand and an ear. Brightly coloured boxes on wheels resembling chariots pass to and fro at an alarming speed, but they are not pulled by horses. It is impossible to know how they are powered. The air around them is thick and choking. Is no one aware of that?

All around me there are harsh noises, but the aliens appear not to notice. They are all confined in their own personal worlds, isolated, disconnected. Oh, look – perhaps this is a dwelling, again another box. Let me peep inside through this hole in the wall. Here is a box-like room, occupied by a group of aliens sitting together. They seem to be intently watching yet another box. This one has a polished surface like a stone, but with very small aliens imprisoned inside it. Is this some sort of punishment for crimes they have committed? And are the aliens who are watching the small prisoners also being punished? They seem to be incapable of movement, or thought, or speech.

Everything seems suddenly blurred. Oh, oh, my head – it's splitting! The sun is rising in the sky. Have I been dreaming? Have I seen a ghastly future? Oh dear, I'm surrounded by heaps of half-consumed poppies. Opium is such a bad habit! I must try to give it up. Let me quickly gather my tools together. It's almost time to join the team building the Great Wall that protects China from the Mongols.

A REVELATION?

Making earnest progress through the crowded shopping centre was a young man, tall, upright, with a clean-cut square jaw, wide-open blue eyes and an abundance of fair hair.

During his service training, he had suffered harsh conditions in Norway, living in a shelter carved with his own hands from the snow and ice. Together with his team he had dug out survivors of mudslides in Bangladesh, and erected temporary shelters for victims of tropical hurricanes and other natural disasters.

Rightly proud of his accomplishments, he served his country gladly. Each November he took part in the memorial parades, immaculate and upright in his service uniform.

The young man's earnest progress through the crowded shopping centre came to an abrupt halt. Whose was that face staring so fixedly at him? Somehow it resembled a large walnut with dewlaps. There were two slits where the eyes should have been, and there was a white tuft of hair just above the forehead.

Grandpa bit his lip, and shrugging his shoulders continued his earnest progress through the crowded shopping centre.

That reflection in the shop window had nothing to do with him.

THE RECORD PLAYER
*Fiction based on historical facts,
not to be taken seriously*

On Tuesday 25 July 1911 the archaeological world was agog with the news that the American historian Hiram Bingham on the previous day had discovered Machu Picchu, an ancient Inca settlement on top of a mountain in Peru. The name was locally understood to mean 'old peak'. The site itself was considered to be intact, and not a pile of ruins.

Having acceded to the British throne on 6 May 1910, George Frederick Ernest Albert, crowned as King George V, was anxious that Britain should remain a powerful influence in the world. Accordingly, he arranged for a team of well-respected archaeologists to be despatched to Peru to see if other important ruins of the Inca race could be discovered. He was keen that Britain should not be eclipsed by the Americans, even if there was a 'special relationship' perceived between the two governments. However, this project promoted by the King himself was purely speculative, and it was envisaged that it would cover some years with no guarantee of success.

Among the members of the team despatched to Peru was Graham Inchbold, who was not only an eminent archaeologist, but also an internationally recognised expert on the translation of ancient languages.

The British team was blessed with good fortune much sooner than expected, and in the heat and dangers of the Peruvian jungles unearthed the ruins of what appeared to be a temple. After a short examination of the tangled remains, a large, heavily ornamented marble slab was uncovered, with an inscription in a language that Graham Inchbold did not recognise. Delirious with delight, he was allowed to take this irreplaceable piece of treasure home to

Buckinghamshire, where he began the immense task of hopefully translating the unrecognised ancient language.

Many hours of diligence achieved some progress, producing a partial translation of the wording. The entrancing inscription began with the words 'This temple is dedicated to . . .' The expert's heart began to thump with excitement. Could this be the acme of his career? So much depended upon the meaning of this tantalising inscription. Would he discover a tribute to an ancient heathen god? Would he, Graham Inchbold, find the name of a powerful ruler of a hitherto unknown race? Would he be the founder of a whole new branch of history? There were definite prospects for the further enhancement of his already glittering career, perhaps even recognition from the King. Having reached this point of his translation late at night, the renowned expert in ancient languages reluctantly needed to take his rest, resolving to reach the thrilling conclusion of his work the next day.

When the next morning arrived, Graham Inchbold was too excited to bother with a full breakfast, and satisfied himself with a large cup of extra-strong coffee. His hands were shaking with nervous anticipation as he sat down at his desk to gradually reveal the last few words of this ancient message. The eventual revelation was too much to bear. He sprang from his chair, screaming, "No! No! This can't be right!" He began tearing his hair, stamping his feet, grinding his teeth. Then, trying to calm his rage, sat down to check his work. It was right. There was no mistake. He plunged his sweat-covered face into his shaking hands, then, lifting his fevered head, pounded his fists in anguish on his desk, making the knuckles bleed.

This bolt from the blue would mean the complete disintegration of his whole distinguished career, and, worse still, would also lead to the tarnishing of the hitherto brilliant reputation of the archaeological team toiling in Peru at a worthless project. The ancient stonemason who had carved the message so artistically on the beautiful slab of marble was no more nor less than a joker – someone who played with written historical records, someone who had no respect for the past or the future – and he, Graham Inchbold, had become the butt of this warped man's wicked sense of humour.

Having discharged his anger and anguish, Graham Inchbold washed the sweat from his face and the blood from his knuckles. He knew he had to face the truth. He could not claim to the world that he had been unable to translate the dedication on the marble slab. That would be an additional disgrace. He would have to submit to the ridicule he would most certainly receive. Taking the most expensive sheet of paper he could find, in his best calligraphy he wrote out the message he had translated from the artistic carvings of an irreverent player with written records. Standing up, he took all his courage in his hands and addressed an imaginary audience of world-renowned archaeologists and experts in the field of ancient languages, as he would be obliged to do in reality in the near future. In a strong, confident voice, he read out his translation:

"This temple is dedicated to those who died building it."

BEGINNING ON THE MAJOR ROAD AHEAD

We start in mist; this road's not ours;
It leads within another's powers.
The mist will clear – which road to choose?
On one we gain, another lose.

Our map will show us rough terrain,
But cannot forecast sun or rain.
We travel on and soon we find
This road's one-way and closed behind.

Our major road will come full stop,
And once again the mist will drop.
Beyond the mist is purer air.

Oh! Look!
Our newer life's beginning there.

THE SHOPPING LIST

I came to an abrupt halt at the entrance to the supermarket as a feeling of alarm spread over me. I began to rummage in my handbag. No, nothing. Again, in my coat pockets, nothing. And nothing at all in the shopping bag. Where was that list? Had I left it in the fridge, the tumble dryer? At this late stage in life, anything was possible.

Feeling rattled, I decided to sit on a sunny bench overlooking the rock-strewn River Erme and consider what I might have written on my missing list. A bottle of Veuve Clicquot champagne, one kilogram of Black Summer Italian truffles from Umbria, a large joint of ostrich meat, fresh yaks' milk from the foothills of the Himalayas? I did not feel absolutely confident that the local supermarket could provide those items. In fact, it was more likely that I needed a bottle of bleach, a handful of mushrooms, some Quorn mince and some soya milk.

Remembering the familiar words from the well-known song 'Scarborough Fair', I wondered if I needed herbs. Parsley, sage, rosemary and thyme?

"There's rosemary for remembrance."

Thank you, Ophelia and Hamlet – I could use a memory jolt.

"Parsley for bitterness."

The only bitterness I felt at that moment was caused by the loss of my shopping list.

"Sage for strength and wisdom."

Oh, yes please – how helpful that would be!

"Thyme for courage and happiness."

That is a universal need, I thought.

What else did the young jilted lady require from her lost love who once lived at Scarborough Fair? All sorts of things impossible

*The author contemplating her shopping list by the River Erme.
Photograph by Phillip Frank Dredge.*

to achieve, including the return of his affections. This wish list was of no further help for me.

Sitting comfortably in the sunshine, I remembered another wish list composed by Wilfrid Wilson Gibson called 'The Ice Cart':

> *And I was wandering in a trice
> Far from the grey and grimy heat
> Of that intolerable street
> O'er sapphire berg and emerald floe
> Beneath the still cold ruby glow
> Of everlasting Polar night,
> Bewildered by the queer half-light,
> Until I stumbled unawares
> Upon a creek where big white bears
> Plunged headlong down with flourished heels
> And floundered after shining seals
> Through shivering seas of blinding blue.
> And, as I watched them, ere I knew
> I'd stripped and I was swimming too.*

I resisted the urge to plunge into the River Erme. For one thing, I can't swim.

Well, the local supermarket wouldn't be stocking a sapphire berg or an emerald floe either. Reluctantly, I struggled to my feet and, heading to the store once again, I settled for the bottle of bleach, the handful of mushrooms, the Quorn mince and the soya milk.

PUNCTUALITY

When I tell you that I can say "I'm sorry I'm late" in five different languages – French, Italian, German, Dutch and, of course, English – that will immediately give you some indication of my character.

Has the human race been cursed with a form of punctuality from the very beginning? Did a form of punctuality arrive with Adam and Eve in the Garden of Eden? It is said that the blackbird is the first to greet the dawn with its own particular hymn of thanks and praise, and apparently the daisy is the first flower to unfurl its petals at the hint of daylight, for that reason being originally called 'the day's eye'. Do the blackbird and the daisy have a dawn tryst on dark and cold drizzly days? Are they punctual? Only they would know.

Who *was* that rogue who invented punctuality? I think that person was an anxious, impatient, fidgeting finger-twiddler and toe-tapper who could not bear to see anyone else at ease. If that person would make himself known, I would congratulate him by warmly grasping his throat.

Some method of measurement is necessary to achieve punctuality. The ancient Egyptians – Nefertiti, Tutankhamen, Akhenaton and their various clans – divided the hours of their days by observing the noiseless, shifting shadows formed by their obelisks. How wonderfully inexact! How wonderfully civilised!

The ancient Romans and Greeks had a similar idea with their sundials, which were couched in artistically created, peaceful gardens. Why not bring them back?

By the time the Middle Ages had arrived in Northern Europe, punctuality had been in the wings for a while, quietly anticipating its fledging – the religious orders had been entrusted with timekeeping. Their magnificent bells rang out the call to prayer at midnight for matins; lauds at 3 a.m., or dawn; prime around 6 a.m.; tierce around 9 a.m.; sext at midday; none around 3 p.m., vespers around 6 p.m., or after dinner; and compline around 9 p.m., or before bed. The only way that farmers or peasants working in the fields could know the time was by listening to the bells. And how precise were they? I wonder.

Which enterprising soul was it who encapsulated that sound of bells in a tin and called it an alarm clock!

It was apparently in the mid-fourteenth century that there was born what I personally would call the Movement of the Megalomaniac, still in force today. The human race must be controlled at all costs for every second of the day. Behold the arrival of the first mechanical clock. Rather like the modern arrival of the Spiraliser or the wok, no life was complete without one. For the first time, it was possible to hold the human race in bondage by measuring time precisely.

The most obvious modern eruption of punctuality was perceived in the Victorian era with the creation and perfection of the steam locomotive. It was a brilliant suggestion that the various time zones in the United Kingdom should be synchronised in order to operate all trains with punctuality. . . . Oh dear, we seem to have hit a snag. . . .

How I long for the days of the blackbird and the daisy!

DROP IN AND DROP OUT

"That one there," said the tall, thin man.

The Governor nodded in agreement. "Come here, boy."

The tall, thin man grabbed me by the scruff of the neck and held me up in the manner of a magician pulling a rabbit out of a hat.

"It's a bit small. Is it strong?" asked the tall, thin man.

"It will do," replied the Governor.

The tall, thin man needed to know something about it in case of future difficulty. The Governor considered the matter.

"Its mother died giving birth to it, and we have no record of its father" was the only information he could provide.

"How much do you want for it?" the tall, thin man was eager to know.

"Ten shillings to you," suggested the Governor.

The tall, thin man offered, hopefully, "Seven shillings, and I'll take it away."

The deal was settled, and I was propelled out of the workhouse into the street.

The tall, thin man pulled me along the pavement faster than my little legs would allow. Eventually we stopped in front of a very large house. The housekeeper answered the pull on the bell.

"I was passing, and thought I'd drop in to see if you needed any help today, Susie," volunteered the tall, thin man.

"Oh, we do, we do, Andy," replied Susie, and I was pushed into what I thought was a palace. The room was beautifully furnished, sunlight pouring in through a wide bay window, and on the floor thick rugs that I could never have dreamed of in the workhouse.

"Move! Stop daydreaming," growled Andy, and he pushed me

towards the fireplace. He began to manoeuvre a white cloth round the hearth. "Take off your clothes!"

I was horrified and afraid.

"I don't want to! Why should I?"

"Don't ask questions, and do what you're told! Take this brush. Keep it above your head." Andy pushed me up the chimney. "Climb up there using your elbows and knees, and brush all the cinders and soot off the bricks!"

I was crying. "It's dark! I'm frightened! Pull me down again!"

Andy's only response was, "Shut up and do what you're told. When you see a bit of daylight, that's the top of the chimney, and you have to come down again."

The chimney was so narrow, and there was a bend. I was stuck. I tried to cry out, but my mouth was full of soot, and I could only choke. Struggling and struggling hard against the bricks I was free again. At last there was a small circle of light above me, and I tried to come down, but that proved even more difficult than climbing up. The brush above my head was continually pouring soot and cinders, still hot from the morning's fire, over my naked body.

Eventually I was able to drop out of the chimney accompanied by a heavy shower of soot and cinders. There I stood, naked, a six-year-old orphan with no one to protect me, no one to take my part. My back was scorched from the hot cinders, my eyes burning, my lungs bursting from lack of clean air, my ears and mouth full of debris, and my elbows and knees covered in blood. I had been sold body and soul for seven shillings as an apprentice to a chimney sweep.

I began to wail. "I'm tired and thirsty! Please can I have a drink of water?"

Susie, the housekeeper, looked at me, her face screwed up with distaste.

"What a disgusting little thing it is!" she said. "It hasn't done its work very well, has it? The Master won't earn very much when he only has one bag of soot to sell. Send the little brat up the chimney again."

Eventually I was able for a second time to drop out of the chimney.

"Put your clothes back on again!" growled Andy.

I was sooty.

"I need a wash! I'm tired and thirsty! I want a drink of water!"

Again, Andy's only reply was "Shut up and do what you're told!"

Andy took me outside and, picking me up, shook me like a dog shaking a rat to loosen the cinders from my hair. And so we continued along the pavement in search of more houses where we could drop in and ask for work.

A HOUSE CALLED WHISPERING TREES
A fairy tale

Charles and Alice had been married for a year, living in rented accommodation. They were not short of love for each other, and not short of optimism for a rosy future together. However, they were short of money.

On this day, the first anniversary of their marriage, as a treat they had arranged with an estate agent to view a house they had seen advertised in their local paper, knowing full well they could never afford it.

The house was approached by a long tree-lined drive. The sudden view of it at the end of the drive took away their breath. From the exterior, it was exactly what they had dreamed of: a Victorian detached double-fronted villa with welcoming bay windows and a porch with stained glass on each side of the door. It goes without saying, that red roses were clinging invitingly to all the available niches.

The interior held no disappointments. The rooms were spacious, still furnished with the original decorated fireplaces, and the coving and decorations on the ceilings were still intact and artistic. However, the house provided all the modern requirements and it seemed to be saying, "I know you love me. I'm yours! I'm yours!"

If only!

The impecunious couple tore themselves away, taking their empty pockets with them. As they closed the gate at the end of the drive, Charles noticed a copper plate hanging off its fixings. He straightened it, and read the name: 'Whispering Trees'.

"What a lovely name!" they both exclaimed.

At home in the evening, Charles opened the newspaper and turned to the sports pages. He scanned them lazily. Then, suddenly, as if he were suffering a fit, his eyes popping, he threw the paper down and raced to the phone. Alice stared in alarm, but Charles offered no explanation.

The next evening, after their meal, Charles listened to the sports news on the radio.

> At this afternoon's races at Newton Abbot, the rank outsider Whispering Trees in the three-o'clock race romped home first at 40 to 1, leading the favourite, Red Rum, by a good length.

"Alice! Alice! Did you hear that? Yesterday I put our savings on that horse Whispering Trees, and it won! It won! We can buy the house we want!"

Oh, what bliss! A dream come true! The two of them pranced a giddy jig in their small rented room.

Along with their growing family, Charles and Alice are living happy ever after now in that wonderful detached Victorian villa called Whispering Trees at the end of the tree-lined drive, never ceasing to give thanks to that magical horse of the same name.

JEALOUSY: FINE FEATHERS MAKE FINE BIRDS.

Even without expensive clothing, this young woman would be beautiful. How old is she? Eighteen? Nineteen? She is seated at a grand piano in a room with furnishings that suggest the home is owned by a wealthy Victorian family. A shaft of sunlight entering the room through generous French windows is catching her thick blond hair cascading like satin against the dark blue of her dress.

The colours of the Turkish rug are picked out like jewels in the sunlight. The mantelshelf behind the piano provides a resting place for candlesticks, sepia photographs of stern-looking bearded patresfamilias, and several china ornaments. In a corner stands a potted dragon plant.

The other occupant of the room has an appearance reminiscent of Whistler's mother. She is dressed in dark-coloured widow's weeds, with her thinning white hair scraped severely back into a bun. She is occupying a large, comfortable armchair with its back to the French windows, listening placidly to her granddaughter's music and watching her dainty fingers pressing the ivory and ebony piano keys.

What fond thoughts are passing through her mind?

'I was young and beautiful myself once,' she is musing, 'with my whole life in front of me. How many more days has the Good Lord allotted to me, I wonder, and how many of them will be useful? I can no longer hope for an active future. All of my achievements are behind me now. My lovely granddaughter has the world within her grasp. She is beautiful, intelligent, talented, and a lack of money will never be her problem. Oh, how I envy her, how I envy her!'

With a satisfied smile, Miranda, the artist, stepped away from her easel.

"Just a bit of softening for the old lady's hair and a bit of highlighting for the Turkish rug!" was her immediate reaction to this new creation.

A picture paints a thousand words.

Chewing the end of her paintbrush, Miranda murmured, "I think I shall call this one *Jealousy*!"

THE ATTIC ROOM
Be careful what you wish for

It was raining in Kidderminster that fateful afternoon. In Worcester Street the door to the auction rooms was invitingly open. Mary had never been to a property auction, but, partly because it was raining and partly because she was curious, she went in and found a vacant seat. Her copy of the catalogue opened immediately and spontaneously at Lot 99, a 1920s detached house needing modernisation, situated in five acres, comprising three reception rooms, a larger than average kitchen, a larder and a downstairs cloakroom. Upstairs were five bedrooms, two of them en suite, and a family bathroom. From the photograph it seemed an attractive proposition.

When the auctioneer reached Lot 99, valued at £200,000, no one rose to the occasion. Several lower prices were offered, to start the bidding, but still there was no interest. When the auctioneer offered his final starting price of £150,000 Mary could not sit still, and for some unaccountable reason felt compelled to make a bid – the only one. The house was hers.

Most people would agree that when spending £150,000 in one go it is advisable to inspect the goods beforehand. Stepping out of her car an hour later, Mary found that the catalogue photograph of her property had been slightly enhanced. Perhaps the house she had bought at a knock-down price was only fit for being knocked down!

Mary was a young married woman with two beautiful children and a substantial inherited personal income, meaning that she had never needed to earn her own living. Never having possessed a strong maternal instinct, she was always grateful when her husband took an afternoon off work to look after the children while she went out to amuse herself. She had frequently wished that she could find her own permanent space to escape from boring domesticity, and suddenly and so unexpectedly here it was.

The interior of the house was not at all what she had anticipated. It seemed that the previous owners had left in a great hurry, leaving all their 1930s-style furniture behind, many years ago. The curtains had been reduced to rags by sunlight. The sofa in the main reception room had originally been upholstered in a blue floral satin material, but was now covered in mildew. The chairs surrounding the dining table in the room adjoining the kitchen had been brutally pushed back, leaving scars on the otherwise handsome parquet floor. The third and smaller reception room had been used as a library, again smelling of mildew. The pantry was filled with tins of food from a bygone age. Mary did not dare to open the meat safe.

The stair carpet was held in place by tarnished brass stair rods. At the top of the stairs was a generous landing leading to the bedrooms. Again the impression was of a hurried exodus. The bedclothes had been flung back as if the occupants had only just left their beds. On further inspection, Mary found that the wardrobes still contained the owners' clothes, obviously of good quality, probably bought in the 1930s.

The fifth bedroom was too small to be accurately described as such, but it contained a spiral staircase that had not been detailed in the catalogue. At the top, Mary found a heavy-looking door. She surmised that the attic behind the door would contain only cobwebs and rubbish, but it would be exciting if she could find a trunk containing who knew what!

The heavy door offered some resistance, but after several minutes of strong persistence it swung open with a groaning and screaming of the rusty hinges. Suddenly Mary was subjected to what felt like a large, strong hand in the small of her back pushing her over the threshold into the attic, and the door clanged shut behind her with more groaning and screaming from the rusty hinges. She stood still for a minute, shaking with fear. In desperation in the dark she groped for the doorknob. There was no doorknob. There was no door.

Bit by bit, the dark room began to disappear as the roof rolled back, revealing an amazingly blue sky and sunshine. The walls of the attic had melted away and she found herself in a garden paradise filled with the fragrances of oranges, peaches, olives, figs and dates. In the middle of these voluptuous fruit trees was a pretty ornamental pool with a fountain. Looking down, she was a little unnerved to see that she had somehow mislaid her shoes, and her naked feet were supporting her on a chamomile lawn.

"Welcome!" said a disembodied Voice. The Voice seemed to wrap Mary in a warm and comforting blanket.

"Where am I?" asked Mary, hardly able to come to terms with her surroundings.

"You are wherever you want to be!" The warm voice seemed to be softly winnowing her hair, massaging her shoulders and back, and caressing her hands. "I heard your wishes, and this is my gift to you – your own Garden of Eden."

Mary was overwhelmed. "But why would you want to give me this exquisite present? Surely you would want something in return!"

The disembodied but comforting Voice replied, "I have chosen you specially from the seven billion inhabitants of this teeming planet to be my companion. You can live here forever, enjoying every luxury, just by keeping me company."

"But I can't stay here forever! I have a husband and children who need me!"

"You will stay here forever! I have chosen you specially!" The Voice seemed to have acquired a slightly sharp edge.

"Surely you must already have some companions?" asked Mary.

"I do," replied the Voice with some irritation.

"Why can't I see them?"

"They choose not to be seen." The Voice was not so warming.

Mary began to feel alarmed.

"I want to go home! I want my husband and my children!"

"You ungrateful guest! Don't you know how ill-mannered it is to throw a gift back in the face of the person who gave it to you?" The Voice was cold, and wrapped itself around Mary like a freezing, strong silk rope.

She began to choke. "I can't breathe!" she gasped.

The roof began to close over the attic, blotting out the amazingly blue sky and sunshine. As the impenetrable darkness fell, the delicious fragrances of the fruit trees were replaced by the stench of mildew.

There was no one to mount an Appeal against the punishment meted out by the rebuffed and bitter Voice, and no one to release Mary from the freezing, strong silk rope that was crushing her life away. There was no one to witness the execution of this punishment as gradually, over time, her bones became indistinguishable from the bones already scattered in the cobwebs and dust on the floor of the attic room.

THE UNVEILING
Fiction based on an historical event

There had been no courtship, no holding of hands, no gazing into each other's eyes, no whispered endearments. The couple about to be married had never previously set eyes on each other.

In the centuries before the miracle of Skype or the intrusion of the telephone, the custom was for the bride to send a miniature portrait of herself to her intended groom. In this particular case, the portrait emphasised an abundance of fair wavy hair, but other details were strangely blurred. Nevertheless, the prospective groom had kept the image of his bride close to his heart, as any lover would.

Guests were assembling excitedly in the abbey. The groom was impatient to inspect the lady assigned to him. The lady herself was an intelligent young woman, not especially well educated, but generally regarded as gentle, virtuous and docile. What more could any man want!

She had travelled hundreds of miles for her marriage, the last of them across a turbulent sea in conditions somewhat short of P&O comfort. There had been no question of a bended knee accompanied by a protestation of unworthiness on the part of the hopeful bridegroom. The lady had not been required to give acceptance of her groom's proposal of marriage. She had understood from a very young age that she would be given away, with or without her own approval.

There was a disturbance at the entrance to the abbey. The bride and her attendants had arrived. The groom turned to assess his lady. He was delighted to note that she was apparently not a bag of bones. As the ceremony progressed, so did his ardour. He was impatient to crush this voluptuous woman in his arms. However, bearing in mind his surroundings, he desisted.

At last, the longed-for words were pronounced: "Those whom God hath joined together let no man put asunder." The groom was invited to kiss the bride.

The bride did not seem eager to lift her veil for the kiss. There was a rustling and a murmuring among the congregation. Eventually, her attendants slowly and with difficulty raised the thick and heavy material that had hidden her features.

The bridegroom staggered, his knees gave way, he gasped for breath, but not from passion. The woman who had just promised to love him, comfort him and be faithful to him as long as they both should live and would, he had hoped, eagerly, sweetly and passionately provide any number of children for him, finally revealed her features.

She had the face of a horse.

Alone that night in her bedchamber, Anne of Cleves, the twenty-four-year-old former German princess, now the uncrowned Queen of England, the fourth wife of Henry VIII, offered up a fervent prayer: "*Gott in Himmel*, thank you for the ugly face that was unveiled today; thank you for the ugly face that saved me."

THESE FIGURES DON'T STACK UP

The managing director, Duncan MacDiddle, affectionately known by his employees as Drunken MacDiddle, was concentrating hard. He was sitting well back in his expensive rhinoceros-hide chair, his elbows on the arms, his fingertips pressed hard together and pointing to the ceiling. His attention was directed to the set of annual accounts on his desk.

"These figures don't stack up," he said, addressing his financial director.

"They're not meant to" was the reply.

The financial director, Rupert, could afford to be familiar with the managing director, since they were brothers and they ran the MacDiddle Whisky Distillery together, with vague competence and with complete charm, totally dependent upon each other.

"The purchase ledger seems overloaded. I see you have authorised the purchase of a new mash tun. Since they are made of solid good-quality metal, I don't understand how they can wear out."

"Well, it's not a replacement; it's an additional item. We need it to meet the increased demand."

"I haven't noticed an increased demand. Where is it coming from?"

"Well, it's mainly from the employees. They are still enjoying their morning and afternoon half-hour whisky breaks. And our new product development manager seems to have a creative bent, testing his inventions based on expensive ingredients. Your own unpaid-for consumption of our product seems quite high."

"Ah, yes! Our own consumption!" Duncan picked up his telephone. "Mary, bring in the tea trolley, please. We'll have the pint-sized best china tankards, the large coffee pot, some biscuits, and an unopened bottle of our best Welsh whisky. Now, where were we, Rupert?"

"You were looking at the accounts for the year just gone."

"Ah, yes. Salaries look a bit high. Why are we paying our sales manager so much? And, by the way, what is his name?"

"He claims his name is Riddle, but I can't seem to trace his previous employments. He seems a bit of a shady character, but as well as the product development manager he also seems to have a creative bent. He's brought in a lot of revenue, but I'm not quite sure where it comes from. I don't dare ask him. He seems to have some connections in Sicily. From what I read in the newspapers, the island appears to be largely under the control of the Mafia. We don't seem to export enough there to warrant the amount of income that comes back. We're paying him that attractive salary in the hope that he will keep his mouth shut. Ah, here comes Mary with the trolley! Oh, those biscuits look tempting! Thank you!"

The two brothers were spending some pleasant minutes in enjoying their half-hour whisky break when they heard a tremendous metallic crash accompanied by the sound of smashing china.

"That's Mary again," observed Rupert. "When she has finished her own half-hour whisky break, she can't always see very well, and instead of taking the lift back to the kitchen she attempts to push the trolley down the stairs."

Duncan examined the purchase ledger again. "That would explain why you have authorised the purchase of nine additional tea trolleys during the last year, and nine sets of Crown Derby best china. Let's have a look at the sales ledger. Not much doing there. Is Sicily the only place where we sell our product?"

"I'm afraid so," replied Rupert. "Most of our product goes to our employees for their two daily half-hour breaks. Then quite a large percentage goes as free samples to the town councillors. It makes them so happily fuddled that they haven't noticed we haven't paid them any rent for our premises for the last ten years. Our product development manager is hoping to increase income by creating new products. The employees have been testing his Welsh Whisky Bara Brith for some time, so there isn't any actually for sale. The cost of the ingredients is quite high, as you will see from the purchase ledger. At the moment, they are also testing the new Scotch Whisky Tea Bread. That's quite expensive to make as well." Rupert continued: "As you will see, we don't seem to have made much profit this year. After we make allowance for your own modest bonus, which you magnanimously share with me, then take out the generous salary paid to our sales manager to keep his mouth shut, then the mythical rent that we pay to the town council, followed by the cost of our quality ingredients, etc., etc., there isn't a lot left. Talking of bonuses, I have given the usual annual talk to the employees, explaining with a lot of technical detail how extravagantly they are rewarded for their work in keeping the company afloat, and they are quite happy to continue without a bonus, still working to the payment terms and conditions they signed ten years ago."

"I see," answered Duncan. "I take it that this is the creative set of accounts that you intend to send to Companies House and the Inland Revenue, showing them that since we have made only £1,000 profit over the whole year we have no legal obligation to pay tax? We have to show a profit of some kind, or I'm afraid some authority or other will attempt to close us down."

"Naturally," smiled Rupert.

"Then show me the true set of accounts. Aha – as I expected, our loss this year is even greater than it was last year. So we shall need to publish your creative set of accounts this year as usual."

"Yes, I think that figures," replied Rupert.

The two brothers, having completed their tasks for the day, once more resorted to the large coffee pot, the bottle of best Welsh Whisky and the Bara Brith prepared generously with the distillery's best product. Figures are largely hypothetical after all, aren't they?

POSTSCRIPT

The flowers are always fresh. Someone remembers him. Someone loves him enough and cares enough to regularly replace the flowers in the little metal vase attached to the brass plaque. The wording on the plaque comes straight to the point:

In Memory of Charles Cameron, beloved Father and Grandfather,
who used to enjoy sitting here on sunny afternoons.
19th January 1899 to 27th March 1976.
Resting in the Arms of the Angels.

Surely there must be more! Surely during his seventy-seven years he must have achieved more than just becoming a 'beloved Father and Grandfather'! If only the bench could speak!

Charles Cameron was propelled bewildered and gasping on 19 January 1899 into a poverty-stricken slum in Glasgow. As he grew older, he acquired a grim determination to improve his prospects and his life. In desperation as a sixteen-year-old he had left his factory life behind in search of adventure, and had volunteered for the armed forces. Before long, he found himself in even worse circumstances, saving the lives of his wounded colleagues by driving an ambulance through the muddy fields of France.

It was during this time that he met his future wife, a young nurse in the field hospital. At the end of the war they embarked on a new life together in England, and, wounded and gassed, Charles Cameron made what living he could. The years of the Depression intervened, but Charles and Dorothy, his wife, pursued their lives together with the courage and enterprise that had carried them through the war. Sadly they were parted by Dorothy's early death, and Charles began to take his memories to the bench on the cliff overlooking the sea, where on a sunny afternoon he made his final journey to the arms of the angels.

Chattering visitors now take advantage of the sunny bench. Their uninformed and careless backs will polish the brass plaque until eventually the wording will become blurred and lost. The metal vase will become empty and forgotten. There will no longer remain a 'Memory of Charles Cameron, beloved Father and Grandfather, who used to enjoy sitting here on sunny afternoons', no longer a memory of the quiet, determined and courageous man who had made the best of his deprived beginnings and shown bravery in the face of adversity.

Such is the afterthought, the postscript, to the life of an unknown man called Charles Cameron.

Memories on a bench at the seaside.
Photograph by the author.

WANDERING

On that very special day the soft September sun was smiling on Sorrento. Edgar was making determined progress down the hill towards the sea. He was a vigorous-looking young man of twenty-five. His pale face, blue eyes and generous endowment of blond hair proclaimed his Englishness.

As he made his way, he constantly repeated quietly to himself, "Today is the day! Today must be the day!"

He had made his decision.

She was waiting patiently for him, leaning against the railing on the seafront, the love of his life, his destiny. His strong young hand reached out for hers, and she eagerly succumbed to his kisses.

In the Bay of Naples, the soft September sun was smiling on the sea. Its gentle foam-topped ripples seemed to be whispering "Yes-s-s-s-s, yes-s-s-s-s, yes-s-s-s-s" as they sucked at the sand.

Ah, this is the moment, this is the moment.

"Anna, Anna, you know how much I have loved you ever since the moment I first set eyes on you," he murmured into her luxuriant black hair.

"EDGAR! ED-GAR!"

His wife's voice cut through the room like an iced meat cleaver. With difficulty, Edgar hoisted himself up straight in his large, comfortable armchair. It was placed too near the coal fire, and a smell of scorching was rising up from his trouser leg. The biting January wind was flying unfettered across the Cambridgeshire Fens, blowing smoke down the chimney and into the room. Edgar's frail, shaking hand reached up and brushed away the few white wisps that remained of his youthful abundant blond hair. In mid-sentence he stopped murmuring and hauled himself into the present.

"Yes, Jennifer, my sweet, what is it?"

"Oh, Edgar, you're wandering again."

WAXING LYRICAL
A love song

Sunshine was permeating every crevice of the streets, and throughout the town window shutters were closed to keep out the heat. Most of the inhabitants of Brescia were unconsciously enjoying siesta. In one building, however, a particular mind was actively working – a mind that was not entirely at ease.

The owner of the mind, a middle-aged man, had been sitting for several minutes in silent contemplation and admiration of the utter beauty that was confronting him. Tears were beginning to channel his cheeks. The hour of separation, of parting for ever, was fast approaching.

The source of his admiration had a purpose – a purpose that he personally could not fulfil – and this was the reason for their imminent separation.

All too soon, the door opened and admitted a young man – a sensitive, fragile-looking young man. He took a few hesitant steps forward, his eyes searching in the peaceful dimness of the room. He came to a sudden stop, dumbfounded by the beauty that was revealed before him.

The older man rose from his seat, greeting his young visitor with a mixture of gratitude and yet regret. The younger man eagerly seized the object of utter beauty that had captivated the older man – the lyre which had had so much love and care dedicated to its creation. The young musician earnestly examined its graceful yet robust construction, caressing its shapely polished outline, and murmuring words of astonishment. The older craftsman had wrought an instrument of incredible desirability.

The young man sat down, cradling his new possession, hardly believing that it now belonged to him. Under his sensitive fingers, the strings produced a lyrical waxing and waning of music, filling the room, and bringing tears again to the craftsman's face. The craftsman, unable to play the instrument he had created, and therefore unable to fulfil its purpose, and the musician, unable to create the source of his delight, but exquisitely fulfilling its purpose, together made the perfect combination in the peaceful dimness of that room in Brescia.

Author's Note:
Brescia is a city in the northern Italian region of Lombardy. Internationally renowned precious stringed instruments have been fashioned there since the sixteenth century.

A WILD NIGHT IN MALLORCA
Fiction based on a true memoir

At one o'clock one morning in January 1839, moonlight was stuttering through shoals of black clouds driven by the gusting winds that were sending dense whirlpools of rain rebounding from the rooftops of Mallorca. Most citizens were wrapped up in their beds, trying to ignore the noises of the storm outside. However, candlelight could be observed fluttering across the windowpanes of an upper room where a slightly built man in his early thirties was pacing the floor, his mood mimicking the turbulence outside. Being of an artistic nature, he was desperately and apparently ineffectively calling upon his Muse to inspire him.

His young companion, to whom he was not married, as befitted the Bohemian lifestyle adopted by serious students of the arts, was sleeping peacefully in a room on a floor below, together with her two children. The four of them had escaped to Mallorca from Paris hoping to find the warmer weather that might improve the young man's poor health.

Feeling irritable because of his lack of inspiration, the composer sat down at the Pleyel piano he had had specially imported from Paris. His fingers brushed the keys hopefully, and involuntarily the little finger of his left hand began to move in time to the bass rhythm of the rain striking the metal pipe outside the window – beat-beat-beat-beat. His Muse, roused from her slumber, smiled at him. The fingers of his right hand began to form the rise and fall of a melody complementing the sound rising from his left hand. The young man's mood lifted, and soon he became unconscious of the tempest outside, living only in the harmonies evolving from his piano.

As the fluttering of the candlelight began to fade, the young man began feverishly looking for some means of writing down the music that his Muse had inspired in him. By the time the candlelight had failed and the darkness outside the window had begun to peter away, a manuscript had been completed, and the exhausted but fulfilled composer flung himself on to the bed in a corner of the room, not thinking or caring about dressing in his nightclothes.

Later that morning, his mistress, Aurore, brought him back to consciousness with some strong coffee.

"Couldn't you sleep, dear?" she asked. "Did the storm keep you awake?"

"Listen to this, Aurore" was the response, and the young man, having had so little sleep, tumbled off his temporary bed and lurched towards the piano. His sleepiness dissipated as his fingers once again caressed the keyboard, and soon the harmonies and melodies coaxed out of him by his Muse filled the room.

Aurore was entranced.

"Oh, that is so beautiful! How gifted you are! How lucky I am that we met! Oh, do let me listen again!"

Encouraged by Aurore's enthusiasm, her consort wrote the title of his composition at the top of the manuscript:

'Prelude in D Flat Major – The Raindrop'
by Frédéric Chopin.

Author's Note:
Chopin's mistress was Aurore Dudevant, an author writing under the name of George Sand.

'The Raindrop Prelude' was published in 1839 with others of Chopin's Preludes. George Sand recorded in her memoirs that the piece was written during a storm.

THE PIANO
Fiction based on historical facts

In the autumn of 1893, at the age of thirty-six, Henry Wright decided that he no longer needed to earn a living, and in celebration of that happy decision he had an elegant villa designed for himself, his wife and their nine children. When the building was completed in August 1894, the whole family moved into their new home on the 18th of that month, calling it 'Greenhill Villa'. However, their new lives were not without tragedy. Their dearly loved daughter Maisie, a gifted pianist, died of tuberculosis at home at the age of thirteen.

During the following years, the house changed hands five times, until on 26 July 1935 my parents, Elsie May and Frederick, made it their home with other members of my mother's family. My sister Hazel was born there in January 1937, and I made my own appearance in January 1946.

During our older lives, my sister several times told me that she had frequently felt a melancholic presence in the house, particularly when she was playing the piano.

The piano Hazel played was placed in a corner of the smallest downstairs room. It was evidently old, with a completely black outer case supporting two candle holders. The ivory keys were yellowed and chipped at the edges. Nevertheless, the keys were very responsive, with a sweet tone under my sister's clever fingers. I have a feeling the instrument had been left there by Henry and Florence Wright on their removal from Greenhill Villa in December 1911 after the death of their daughter Maisie. Perhaps they would have found it too upsetting to be reminded of their tragic loss each time they looked at it. My sister and I found several objects that had obviously been left behind by that family, additionally unwanted by succeeding families, including a rocking horse in the cellar.

One night, being unable to sleep, Hazel thought that she would like to read, but discovering she had left her book in the piano room she tiptoed quietly down the stairs to retrieve it. As she turned to leave the room, she had an unsettling feeling that she was not alone, and once again experienced the strange melancholic atmosphere that persistently surrounded the piano. Unnerved but curious, she sat down on the sofa and waited.

As she waited, Hazel froze to see a fragile-looking young girl with long ringlets, dressed in pale green, glide noiselessly into the room. Without looking round, she sat down at the piano and began playing soundlessly. As she stroked the keys, she seemed to be whispering, "Piano! Piano! Softly! Softly!"

How long were those two young girls together in the room, without acknowledging each other's presence?

As dawn began to pervade the room, the young girl at the piano slowly faded into the greying shadows, leaving the room to my sister and her strange feeling of melancholy.

Greenhill Villa.
Photograph by Phillip Frank Dredge.

SUSPENSE
Fiction based on an actual trial

Although it was still early morning, the sun slanting through the courtroom windows was troublesome to the 500 and more citizens who had assembled to witness the trial. Birdsong outside the building filtered through this silent crowd.

"You are hereby charged with blasphemy and inciting the inhabitants of this city state to rioting against its government. How do you plead?"

The accused, a grey-haired man of seventy, was seated on a dais, thus allowing everyone in the room to see him. This was no ordinary criminal. He was a well-respected teacher, a kindly and generous man with an innovative mind – a man who had revolutionised the study of the natural world around him. He sat quietly, dignified and self-contained, willing to suffer during the many hours that he knew the trial would last that day.

His three accusers were each allowed an hour to state his case. The accused was allowed an hour to defend himself. The heat in the room increased and became wearying.

In this court it was not the custom for the jury to retire to consider their verdict. Instead, they listened attentively to the evidence placed before them, each making up his own mind as to its validity.

As the evidence ended, the stifling heat of the sun pouring through the windows, emphasised by the number of spectators crushed into the room, added to the feeling of suspense. In many minds, the accused was not a traitor to the city state, but its benefactor, its leading light. The jurors slowly began their voting, each placing a counter into an urn marked 'Guilty' or 'Not guilty'. The 500 citizens and more watched and waited in an air of anxiety and uncertainty. Evident and great reluctance to pronounce the verdict produced silence for a few minutes. Even the birdsong seemed to have faded. Then the word

'Guilty!' was launched into the oppressive and suffocating heat of the courtroom.

There was an uneasy shuffling. The accused was a popular figure among many of the 500 and more citizens who had gathered in the room. The suspense increased as, according to the custom of the courtroom, the accused was asked to name his own punishment. His astonishing words, delivered with firmness and self-assurance, were greeted at first with disbelief, and then with grief and wailing.

The trial was over. The room began to empty. The 500 and more citizens, many unable to subdue their tears, trickled away into the relentless heat of the sun.

Left in the courtroom, surrounded by his weeping friends, Socrates drained the cup of hemlock. Far too soon, the poison reached his heart, and the great man had gone. The suspense of those stifling hours had finally melted away into profound sorrow.

NO DESIRE PATH

There is no ace in the hand that has been dealt to us.
No one can win.
I'm leaving you.

No roll of the dice can take us back to square one,
To begin again.
I'm leaving you.

On our special day, the church was full
Of flowers, of singing, of smiling, of sunshine.
We were young.
I'm leaving you.

We were young.
We made our vows. They were heartfelt.
They had no reality then.
Now I'm leaving you.

We said, "Till death us do part."
It held no reality then.
We were young.
I'm leaving you.

We have followed the same road.
Now it divides.
Your road is hard and solitary.
My path is soft and effortless.
I'm leaving you.

I have no desire to follow this path.
It leads to nothingness. I'm afraid.
I'm slipping away. Hold my hand. Don't let me go.
I don't want to leave you.
I don't want to leave you.

THE TRAY
A parody, not to be taken too seriously!

The house is a very imposing sight as you turn the corner of the long drive leading up to it. It is owned by a self-made man, Alfred Shaw, who employs two dedicated gardeners to surround his home with artistically designed lawns and flower beds.

Today the June sunshine has invited the owner's family to sit outside for their afternoon tea. A capacious table, dressed with a crisp, white broderie-anglaise tablecloth, has been set up at the edge of one of the lawns in the shade of a walnut tree.

It is four o'clock. Alfred Shaw's family have made their way to the table. Alfred himself is sitting, as befits an important family man, at the head of the table. To his right is his twenty-two-year-old son-in-law Henry, a serious young man who wishes to make his way in the world, and the two of them are discussing Alfred's successful business.

Alfred's wife, Elizabeth, a well-preserved woman of forty, is sitting to his left. She is a doting grandmother to the baby placed on her left in a high chair. Sitting next to the baby is its mother, Charlotte, the eldest of two daughters. She is unmistakeably her mother's daughter, with her dimpled cheeks and chestnut-coloured hair.

At Charlotte's side is her younger sister, Annabelle, who has invited her young man, Charlie, to be inspected by her parents. She is busy making sheep's eyes at his handsome young face, and enjoying secretive footsie with him under the table.

Seated at the end of the table is the youngest child, Alastair, and two of his cousins. These three are in their own private world, earnestly discussing a new book, *One Hundred-and-One Things a Young Boy Can Do with a Box of Matches*.

So which member of this genteel gathering is the murderer? Murderers and terrorists belong to two distinct groups. Terrorists are easily recognisable, but murderers display no obvious traits and blend discreetly and quietly into their own particular society. Murderers do not necessarily have green-hued faces or possess a forked tongue. They don't usually burst into a sitting room sporting a gun holster on each hip and crying out, "Stick 'em up!" They don't walk into a dining room bearing a blowpipe equipped with a poisoned dart hidden in a sleeve. No, they are much more intelligent and subtle in their approach.

Now at last the tea tray is approaching. It is so large and heavily laden that the maid needs to push it on a trolley. The tray has a fresh and innocent appearance. But can it actually be transporting the subtle murderer's means of execution? Can the sandwiches made up of cucumber, or ham and tomato, or cheese and salad, be hiding a dose of botulism? Can the jug of Pimms and pineapple be laced with leaves of hemlock masquerading as harmless herbs? There is also a pot of Darjeeling tea – or are those supposed tea leaves really digitalis? Do those sugar lumps hide pinpricks that could really be where cyanide has been injected? There are so many tools of destruction lying on this well-stocked tray, and yet – it looks so innocent!

Well, it is now six o'clock and the sun is losing its power. The baby is still gurgling. No one has jumped up from the table flourishing his or her hands in the air, only to fall dead, face first into the bowl of jelly. No one is writhing in silent agony on the lawn. No one is sprawled backwards, foaming at the mouth and gesticulating wildly. No one is spurting blood across the table. Everything is boringly normal.

In the unlikely event that Agatha Christie, or Sir Arthur Conan Doyle, or any other well-known writer of detective fiction, had been present at this family afternoon tea party, they would have been deeply disappointed in such an unimaginative and happy crew. There will be no murder today. And that tray, so seemingly innocent, but empty now, is apparently what it at first was assumed to be – innocent!

SILENCE

Outside the window there was not a breath of wind to lighten the heavy atmosphere. The room inside was in complete stifling silence, with not even the ticking of a clock. The young man at the window turned towards the room. His shoulders were hunched, his overall appearance one of despair as his eyes searched the floor for an answer to his pain.

He looked up hopefully at the young face opposite him, his fingers twitching in agitation.

"How many times have I told you how sorry I am? I can't tell you again!"

The young woman remained silent, her lips in a half-smile as if the young man's apology was expected, but was nevertheless worthless.

"Speak to me! Speak to me! If only you could speak to me!"

The room remained in stifling silence.

"If only you could tell me you forgive me!"

No words of forgiveness, nor words of recrimination, nor words of comfort emerged from the young woman's half-smiling lips.

The young man returned his handkerchief to his pocket. The guilt hanging so wretchedly on him would not be dissolved through tears. He had missed all his chances of reparation, and now he knew that it was too, too late for any consolation to be offered. Without another glance at the young, half-smiling face, he rapidly left the silent room.

The young woman with the half-smiling face remained still silent in the room, her whole life reduced to grey shadows on a piece of paper in a photograph frame on the mantelshelf.

THE PENITENT

When from my mother I was torn
I did not ask why I was born.
I grabbed my life with both my hands
And built it all on shifting sands.

Without one selfless glance behind
I seized it all. Oh, I would shine!
The pearl within my oyster world
Slipped through my fingers, tainted, knurled.

I'd taken all that life could give
Without a thought that I should live
With due respect for those who shared
Their lives with me, or those who cared.

If I could live my life again,
Would I do better now than then?
But to one life we are confined.
We can't go back. We can't rewind.

Dear God, when You look down on me,
What do You hear, what do You see?
One released from deep despair.
I've learned to love; I've learned to care.

THE SPARK PLUGS OF INSPIRATION

How capricious, how treacherous are those spark plugs of inspiration, the Muses! They may suddenly arrive with the wind or the rain, slipping seductive suggestions into the senses of human beings, and then just as suddenly vanish with the wind or the rain. Being free spirits, they owe allegiance to no one, seeming sometimes impervious to the entreaties of wretched humans for the glimmer of inspiration so necessary for the achievement of their next great creation.

How do we address these elusive beings? The Ancient Greeks had names for the nine goddesses, and ascribed a different talent to each. Perhaps Dante Alighieri in the early fourteenth century implored Calliope, the Muse of epic poetry, to support him as he composed the three books of his political satire, *The Divine Comedy*. Did Richard Wagner beg the assistance of Euterpe, the Muse of music, when he embarked on the four operas that comprise 'The Ring Cycle'?

Even in modern times we hear the desperate exclamation, "The Muse has left me!" as if we honestly believe in the reality of these mythical beings.

But if we do believe that these goddesses will help us in our endeavours to create works that will entertain, educate, enrich the lives of humans and additionally withstand the test of time, perhaps we should ask ourselves what rewards the goddesses themselves could expect to receive in return for their eager prompting? They do not need gold or silver or jewels or other earthly material riches to be heaped on them. Their only reward must be the poetry, plays and music that evolve as a result of their mystical presence, and the implied praise that is obviously engendered by the success of each created work.

Where do the Muses go when they disappear? They were born at the foot of Olympus to their father Zeus, 'the father of the gods and mankind', and their mother Mnemosyne (Memory). Perhaps the Muses need to go home to their parents to refresh themselves. Because of their own experience of wandering in far-flung foreign climes, did they inspire the song made popular by Frank Sinatra: "It's nice to go travelling . . . But it's so much nicer, yes, it's oh, so nice to wander back." Do they become homesick? Perhaps they need to enthuse each other with their gifts. What wonderful theatre they must create when they are all together – an enrichment of song, dance, music and speech!

Was it possible that the Muses sometimes enjoyed the company of the sirens, who hypnotised sailors with their enchanting songs, luring them to their death on the dangerous rocks surrounding their island home? Did Euterpe, the Muse of music, teach them the sweet harmonies? Did Melpomene, the Muse of tragedy, give them that murderous idea underlying their entertainment? Did Terpsichore, the Muse of dance and chorus, in company with Thalia, the Muse of comedy, guide the hand of Molière as he composed the ballets and farces that so delighted Louis XIV, but at the same time brought down the wrath of the Catholic Church and other authorities upon his head?

How can we possibly guess or know the real motives that prompt the Muses in their unending, unpredictable and frustratingly sporadic interactions with humankind? Perhaps it entertains them to see what happens when they offer controversial ideas to their naïve and trusting servants!

PROFOUND MOTHER-LOVE
An alternative version of an Ancient Greek Myth

The young man was lying on the ground with his back to the sun at the side of a pool. The sun shining through his golden-blond hair was causing a halo effect around his head. He looked fragile, although his youthful face was very striking. How old was he? Certainly not more than eighteen. How long had he been lying there? Perhaps for the last few days. He appeared to be lost in a fantasy, looking earnestly into the deep, dark waters of the pool, most of the time keeping so still that birds had been perching on his back, then flying away of their own accord, and not from fright. Butterflies had landed on his arms to clean their proboscis with their front legs and fan their wings in the warmth of the sun. Grasshoppers had hopped on to his legs and then hopped away again.

Now and again the young man would stir and dip his fingers into the deep, dark waters of the pool, but whatever his prey may have been it always evaded his hand, and he would lie flat again in an attitude of despair.

Into his reverie filtered the voice of his mother, the nymph Liriope: "Narcissus, where are you? Where are you? Ah, there you are! Have you been here all this time? I've searched everywhere for you!"

The young man did not answer.

His mother, appalled at his poor, wasted appearance, sat down beside him and pulled him towards her. He struggled in her arms as he continued to earnestly probe the deep, dark waters of the pool. His mother saw instantly the reason for her son's hopeless suffering as he desperately thrust his hands into the water. It was obvious from the look on his face and his pitiful attempts to trap the image confronting him that he had fallen in love with his own reflection. But his efforts to catch it repeatedly fractured the surface of the water, causing the beautiful face to elude him time and time again.

Is there anything a loving mother will not do for her child, even to her own disadvantage? How could she help her son to escape his misery? Ignoring his struggles, she pulled him once more towards her. As the nymph tenderly stroked his beautiful but pallid face, his skin gently became waxy and white, the petals of a flower. His golden hair gradually became pollen in the cup of the petals. His slender body became a supple, green stem as his legs became the leaves that would anchor the whole flower to the ground.

Stemming the tears that flowed from her own personal sacrifice, the young man's mother turned and walked away, leaving the beautiful narcissus flower that had once been her fragile son nodding to its reflection in the deep, dark waters of the pool.

MY WONDERFUL MOTHER, MY BEST FRIEND

I don't remember my father. He died of food poisoning when I was a year old. When I had reached an age where I could understand, my mother explained that at the time of his death she was a sweet young thing, and having flashed a winning smile at the coroner he charmingly recorded the event as 'Death by Misadventure'. Well, my father's death turned out to be a blessing in disguise, leaving the pair of us in a well-appointed, mortgage-free home in the New Forest propped up by a substantial bank balance.

At school, I never made any friends. All the other pupils decided right from the very first glance that I was a bit 'odd'. That never bothered me. I had a wonderful close relationship with my mother, and I found that our bond was sufficient for my emotional well-being. In good weather, our favourite activity was to take a full picnic basket and two expensive good-quality shotguns into the forest. Shooting at the heads of grey squirrels proved an interesting challenge. It was difficult first of all to spot them among the foliage and then take quick aim. They were no sooner visible than they had daintily hopped away. Have you ever noticed the way squirrels scamper over open ground? They take a few quick steps, stop for a second while they look around, then take another few quick steps, and so on, with the result that shooting at their heads was so easy it seemed like cheating to shoot them in the open and was much less fulfilling.

As I grew older, my mother was keen to offer me some fond, kind motherly advice. Sometimes she would scrutinise me from head to toe, and after a few moments of contemplation would always come to the same conclusion: "If you ever marry, it will have to be to a man who is blind."

Well, so it turned out. Not only was he blind, but he was also wealthy.

My blind fiancé and I chose to marry on my forty-second birthday. The day turned out to be a bit of a shambles. At the reception, while my new husband and I were dancing, my mother accidentally got her feet caught in my bridal train and unfortunately wrapped it round my husband's ankles. Blind persons very often experience problems with their balance, and my husband fell backwards on to the side table where the wedding cake was displayed. Someone had absent-mindedly left a broken champagne bottle by the cake, and it became embedded in my husband's skull. It took him seven hours to die of blood loss. The cake was a bit of a mess, which was a pity since it had cost a lot of money and had looked delicious.

At the inquest, I flashed a winning smile at the coroner, and he charmingly recorded the event as 'Death by Misadventure'.

Sadly, as my mother grew older, she became cantankerous and finally needed to take to a wheelchair. However much I admired my mother and valued her loving care, I had not been born to deal with such a situation and could not tolerate it for long. Having dismissed my mother's carer, we found ourselves on holiday in a bed and breakfast at Land's End. By the afternoon of the second day, we had settled in and I took my mother in her wheelchair for a breath of fresh air along the clifftop.

The members of the jury looked quite affable, I thought, and on my entry into the court I flashed them a winning smile. I explained fluently how, as I was pushing the wheelchair along the clifftop, I had slipped on a patch of mud, ending up sprawled out full-length, and the wheelchair had whizzed away from me over the edge of the cliff, catapulting over the craggy rocks straight down into the sea. I added that I had been humiliated and shamed as I made my way back to the bed and breakfast caked from head to toe in mud.

I have been detained at Her Majesty's pleasure, although how she obtains her pleasure from my detention is difficult to discern. She doesn't visit me. I am the solitary occupier of this miserable room. Her Majesty must be quite tight-fisted, judging from the quality and quantity of its furnishings. I have a small uncomfortable bed, a rickety old table and an ancient dining chair. There is no armchair, and no television. However, Her Majesty has kindly left me a large quantity of writing paper, some pencils and a couple of Biros on the table. Her thoughtfulness has enabled me to jot down a few fond memories of my mother, and that is how you find me now.

JUST ONCE TOGETHER
A prose poem

Just once together through the open doorway we watched the sun bleed into the sky.

Just once together we heard the voice of the white bellbird chime against the failing light.

Just once together we captured a view of the soundless flight of the owl into the shadows.

Just once together we felt the perfume of the night-scented stock hanging heavy on the still air.

Just once together we caught sight of the glancing glints of moonlight reflected on the sullen waters of the lake below.

Just once together could never be enough.

I held your hand, and wished the night would last forever.

I held you close, as just once together we whispered goodbye.

Goodbye, my precious child, just one day old.

IMPATIENCE

Oh, come, please come; and oh, please make it soon!
Come with the sun, or come under the moon.
Come rain-soaked or windblown, come to my door!
The here and the now is what life is for.

The clock's mean hands deal time in short measure.
The time it spares is our precious treasure.
Waiting is wasting time we could borrow.
We'll have rosebuds now; maybe tomorrow.

So please, oh, please come – share some time with me.
The future is hidden, who sees what will be.
This abyss called longing is but for you.
So hurry, hurry! Time doesn't accrue.

Part Two

Planet Earth

TRUTH UNSUBDUED
A prose poem

Oh, stay, northern sun, stay!
   Don't abandon us too soon!
   Don't cease to bless the landscape with your soothing warmth, radiating from the still-blue sky!

Sahara-seduced swifts and swallows have followed the north-westerlies.
   Their flight has brought closure to Summer's show, leaving me to set nature's stage anew.

From my palette let me toss amber and red to the waiting leaves, and blue, purple and vermilion to the fruits of the hedgerows. So shall I begin in tranquillity, questioning the clamours of southern climes for possession of our weakening northern sun.

But truth cannot remain subdued.

The days of dreaming now are gone.

The Equinox will usher in the gasping gales that scorn the final peaceful days of Summer.
   Greyness will hide the last blue skies, creeping from the gathering twilights spawned by the receding sun.

Rebounding rain will tear down dizzying leaves, preparing the north for its coming rest.

I have begun my task.
   I have a name.
   My name is Autumn.

HELIOS, THE GOD OF THE SUN

This relief was found by Heinrich Schliemann in 1872 at the temple of Athena in Ilion (Troy). The relief is now housed at the Pergamon-Museum in Berlin, Germany. iStockphoto.com 1068058146.

MODERN SUN WORSHIP

Even in these modern times, human beings still worship the sun. Their obeisance is usually visible on a beach, or on a bench in a park, or on a lawn, and dress appears to be optional!

All of the ancient races worshipped the sun, and each race had its own name for that deity. The Ancient Greeks and Romans called their sun god Helios, or Phoebus, or Phoebus Apollo, or Apollo.

In the author's prose poem 'Kaleidoscope' Helios represents the weak northern winter sun struggling to shine through intermittent clumps of cloud. In her poem 'Birdsong' the sun is represented by Phoebus, who is envisaged harnessing his four horses to pull his carriage across the sky, from where his aureole, the sun itself, will light the day.

BIRDSONG

Phoebus knows when it's time of day
To release his steeds from halter.
No starry light will dare to stay,
And darkness cowed must falter.

The blackbird with his sweet alarm
Will arouse his harmonious crew.
The air will swell with joyful charm
As the spring day is greeted anew.

The god will accept such hymn of praise
As he urges his chariot onward.
The skies will reflect his aureole blaze
On a new day declared by a songbird.

Crescendos of birdsong escort the god
On descent from his heavenly highway.
As his chariot slides to its fiery abode
Starry light will depose the spring day.

KALEIDOSCOPE
A prose poem

Hesitant Helios shone warm rays through the silent white world of mist and rime, opening earth's veins to flood the land with green.

Rising higher in the heavens, the sun god smiled on the exuberance he had created, and saw that it was good.

At Summer's end, when Autumn called, the sun god's power began to wane. His dying embers showered down, revealing jewelled colours from the green. The Autumn winds tore leaves from the trees, arranging and rearranging a kaleidoscope of scintillating topaz, fiery ruby, secretive tourmaline, glowing garnet, and shy rose quartz.

Seeing earth's veins exhausted, Winter once more seized his icy wand, spreading wide his silent white world of mist and rime.

EVERYTHING HELD DEAR

Before we go any further, let me make the truth clear, without vanity, without exaggeration, without pomposity. I am the luckiest woman in the whole world. I live in the most beautiful country in the whole world – Italy – and in Italy I live in its most beautiful city. I have everything I want, and much more than I need. I am a successful young businesswoman, deriving a reliable source of income from the block of apartments that I let to respectable tenants, so at the same time I have youth and wealth. My friends tell me I am very attractive. In addition, I have a great deal of freedom, so my life is perfect.

The city that is my home is well planned and contains everything a citizen could desire. We have a theatre, a laundry, at least thirty-three bakeries, an excellent selection of brothels – one on almost every street – and many shops and fast-food outlets. These are particularly useful in the evening, when parties of theatregoers are on their way home after a performance and need a quick snack on the way.

Come with me and look at my home. How cleverly it is designed! It has an upper storey, and its three sides partly surround a shady courtyard where I can entertain my friends and relatives. My villa has every modern luxury available in this city, including its own fresh water supply that allows me to enhance my garden with water features. Look at these exquisite pictures on the walls inside my rooms! I am particularly fond of this still-life painting. How realistic those eggs look! And here is a portrait of two of my very kind neighbours, Paquius Proculo and his wife.

Oh, do excuse me – I am so ill-mannered! I have been talking away and haven't introduced myself properly! My name is Julia Felix, and I live in Pompeii.

This morning something feels wrong. The air is heavy, oppressive.

I did not sleep well last night. One of my neighbours, a magistrate, owns several horses, and all night long I could hear them voicing their anxiety and stamping their hooves. Walking round my garden at dawn this morning, everything was unnervingly quiet. I could not find a trace of birds, butterflies or bees among my flowers, vines and trees. As usual, before breakfast I went to the public women's baths, and talking to my friends and acquaintances I found that they also had an uneasy feeling and were perplexed – their cats and dogs had disappeared. Perhaps their pets were aware of something sinister that we humans were incapable of sensing.

After bathing, I went home for breakfast. My servants (I told you I was wealthy!) had prepared an appetising meal of a wheat pancake with dates and honey for me. But I could not settle. I could not enjoy my meal as I should have. Mount Vesuvius has been groaning and growling for some hours now, throwing out ash and columns of fire. But I am sure it will settle soon and become quiet once again.

Well, it's mid-afternoon now, and I am so afraid. My servants have left me alone in my courtyard. They were afraid too. The growling is louder, and even more hot ash is spewing from Vesuvius. The sun has disappeared, the sky is darkening, and the air is so hot – too hot to breathe. I'm choking! My garden has disappeared! Everything I hold dear has disappeared under a layer of hot ash! It is so dark, so hot! Let me kneel and thank the gods for giving me such a perfect life! But they can't save me! I can't breathe any more! Everything is black! Goodbye! Goodbye!

Author's Note:
Julia Felix was an actual businesswoman who owned a large block of apartments in Pompeii. Her house had a private water supply, and the inner walls of her home were adorned with paintings, *Still Life with Eggs* being one of them.

*A victim of Vesuvius.
Photograph by the author.*

Internal domestic decorations typical of Pompeii. Photograph by the author.

ENGLAND IN MAY

There is no place on earth like England in the month of May. The poet Robert Browning expressed his homesickness in the month of April in his poem 'Home Thoughts from Abroad'. I wonder if he added silently in his mind, 'Oh, to be in England now that May is there.'

The medieval peasant in the merry month of May would give vent to his May-time euphoria by flinging open his doors and windows to let in the breeze fragranced by the flower meadows, letting out the acrid smoke lingering from the tallow candles that had illumined his cold, dark winter home. The song 'Sumer Is Icumen In, Lhude Sing Cuccu!' might have resounded in the May sunlight.

The Yorkshire-born musician and composer Frederick Delius was likewise inspired 'On Hearing the First Cuckoo in Spring', and the English poet Andrew Young, saddened by the transience of spring, noted that 'Though the cuckoos shout, they will forget their name ere June is out.'

Oh, wonderful May, the Month of Inspiration, how you bring this country to life! The Worcestershire poet A. E. Housman, at the age of twenty, lamented that the fifty summers left to him were not enough to spend traversing the woodland ride in search of the cherry tree in bloom. Similarly, I do not find that the thirty-one days of May are sufficient for enjoying this doorstep of summer.

The author's pastiche of springtime flowers.

THE WONDERFUL WINTER MONTH OF JANUARY
A prose poem

From the dark, silent cocoon of December emerges January, the chrysalis of spring.

The elements may hurl themselves against the frozen soil, but the earth is only sleeping, resting.

Bare, black twigs, newly dressed in white, are preparing to flaunt themselves in green, while below in the resting darkness of the earth roots are preparing for their springtime pulsing.

God's humble ploughman, the worm, never sleeps. Below the frozen soil he continues to work in the warmer deeps, preparing for the burst of life that spring will bring.

January, the Month of Promise, will surprise us, bringing forth tender white blooms that can pierce the snow. With them comes hope of life renewed.

January, oh January, you are the best of months!

January blooms – watercolour by the author.

OUT AND ABOUT IN THE WILDS

'I know a bank where the wild thyme blows.' I know the sentinel trees where plundering eagles weave their ragged eyries. I know the windswept heathland where harems of red deer protected by their stags roam the ferns and heather. I know the dense forests where secretive pine martens hide their dens. I know the clear, open waters where joyful otters frolic. I know where barren mountains keep watch over the land, and where deep sea lochs mirror the sky. I can meditate under dim and cool canopies of woodland that harbour mossy floors and birdsong.

I love the untamed Highlands of Scotland, and I love particularly Ardnamurchan, a protected area that is approached only by a single-track roadway, crucially restricting access for human beings. Its forbidding rocky coast is surmounted by a lighthouse and crowded with the ever noisy, ever restless seabirds that find a home in the crags. The surrounding salt waters are home to freewheeling seals. But life is not easy here. The weather is always unpredictable, and sometimes all four seasons can be experienced in a single day! The winters can be long and harsh when layers of snow make food hard to find for wildlife. This is the remote and inhospitable place of my birth and upbringing. It forms part of my nature, part of my heart and soul. I belong to it, and will never wish to leave.

But do not imagine that I am an ordinary Scot. No, far, far from it. There are fewer and fewer like me.

I crave a full moon. I am a solitary soul who savours roaming out and about alone through the northern nights, alert to the fragrances of the countryside, grateful for the touch of the breeze. There is very little in my world that can perturb me.

My neighbours the pine martens are silent, active, nocturnal cat-like animals that rarely reveal themselves. These acrobatic, unpredictable little creatures are endowed with claws that are specially adapted to climbing trees, so although they may be present they remain invisible. They are my competent competition. We search in the darkness for the same prey. Sometimes I will fell a rabbit to take home for a tasty supper. Sometimes I disturb sheltering mice or field voles, or stumble upon carrion left by eagles.

Don't come too close to me. I can't say this brief encounter brings me any joy. You do not belong in my world, and this is my territory. Human beings bring destruction. ***They*** are the intruders. They have almost wiped out my kind. They hunt us mercilessly as if humans and only humans have rights on this planet. Keep your distance. My fangs are deadly. My claws are razor-sharp.

My den lies under this brushwood. My lithe little body can squeeze through the smallest space. Do not attempt to follow. My four wild kittens are crying for me. I have been gone too long.

Authors Note:
'I know a bank where the wild thyme blows' is a line from Shakespeare's *A Midsummer Night's Dream*.

RETURN OF THE PINE MARTEN

The pine marten, a small, wild cat-like animal, is an endangered creature, but great efforts are being made by many organisations, particularly in Scotland, and in Northern Ireland by Queen's University Belfast, to ensure its survival.

The January 2020 edition of *The Countryman* magazine reports that following research carried out by the School of Biological Sciences at Queen's University Belfast it has been discovered that pine martens are highly adaptable, particularly where their diet is concerned.

In January 2020 the Woodland Trust reported that, although in past times this lively and curious animal was widespread across the UK, it has now become restricted to the Scottish Highlands as a result of the destruction of its habitat. The pine marten is now legally protected and is beginning to spread once more across Scotland.

In February 2020, Stuart Edmunds, communications officer, Shropshire Wildlife Trust, reported that the trust had discovered pine martens in 2015 after they were presumed extinct for over a century in the county. Since then, the trust has worked hard to monitor them and work out the population size and their distribution with the aim of raising awareness and ensuring that woodland habitat is protected for them.

RETURN OF THE SCOTTISH WILDCAT

In the *iPaper* dated Wednesday 20 November 2019, the journalist Florence Snead reported on plans to release wildcats into the Scottish countryside in 2022 in a venture to prevent their extinction.

The Scottish Wildcat Conservation Action Plan website reports that animal health and welfare will be taken into account to ensure that there will be no interbreeding with feral domestic cats. The venture is being supported by the European Nature Trust.

WILDCAT

You are alone now, my friend,
Alone in your death as you were in your life.
You were the last of your race,
The lonely one.

I saw you last winter,
The watcher watched.
You crouched in the snow,
Your bones as clear as your sunlit eyes.
You were trembling with expectation,
Your tail flicking, sending showers of snow in a miniature storm,
To form small drifts around your frozen matted paws.

Then you sprang.
You arched through the air, and landed lightly,
Noiselessly. You devoured your meal, a robin.

You were alive then,
As alive as you are dead now.
Then you suddenly sensed my presence.
With flattened ears,
And sunlit eyes as fierce as a blazing fire,
You arched your back, bannered your tail,
And hissed and spat, quivering with terror.
I meant no harm, but you hated all men,
With their traps and guns.
You hated me, and you turned and fled
As fast as your starved and weary frame would let you.

I came back this winter to find you.
I found you, the last of your race.
You were stretched out bleeding in the bespattered snow.
Your beautiful eyes, once so clear and full of sunlight,
Were clouded and sightless.
You were dead, the hunter hunted.
You were dead.
The last of your race.
The lonely one.

EARTH REPLIES TO THE SUN

The earth is in thrall to its solar lord
And, circling, replies to its burning orb.
The daisy replies to the sun on the rise,
And creeping things too as they open their eyes.

Through the daily clatter of life on earth
All things respond to the source of their birth.
When the shadows lengthen birds raise their hymn
Of thanks as the northern sun's rays fall dim.

The sea replies to the beckoning moon
And turns its course to another lagoon.
The southern sky sees the sun on the rise
And earth once again will send its replies.

*The **Blue Lotus Flower** with its stunning blue petals and distinctive perfume has been used since the time of the Ancient Egyptians to induce a relaxed state of mind.*

In its potent state, the flower is an hallucinogen, producing a feeling of euphoria giving rise to hallucinations.

In her poem 'The Needy Lotos-eater', *the author has offered her own pictures of what that experience of lotus-induced hallucinations could resemble.*

THE NEEDY LOTOS-EATER
With my sincerest apologies to Alfred, Lord Tennyson for his poem 'The Lotos-eaters'

Give me yet more of the lotos!
Let me be lost in its spell!
Leave me here on this island
Close to the sea's gentle swell.

Give me yet more of the lotos!
Leave me in peace here to lie
With my body entombed in its fragrance,
And I'll watch the sun shatter the sky.

Give me yet more of the lotos!
My pain has been numbed in its fronds.
As the phoenix can surge from the ashes,
So my spirit will soar from its bonds.

Give me yet more of the lotos!
And then I shall always be free.
Silence and stillness come swiftly
As the sky dissolves into the sea.

The blue lotus flower.
iStockphoto.com 820832956

ALTER EGO – A DREAM

Alter ego, what shall we do
When the moon is bright and full?
Over the meadows and through the shadows
I will bend myself to your will.

I have no choice; I follow your voice.
Your amber eyes will light the way
Over the trees and abbey towers
All through the night and into the day.

Alter ego, what shall we do
When the moon is full and bright?
The hunt is on, we turn and twist,
And swooping low we catch and bite.

As the night fades into grey
We barn owls need to find some rest.
We have hunted; the prey is caught
And we must take to our daylight nest.

Alter ego, what must I do
Now that the airborne dream is dead?
The fantasy all too soon has ended
And I turn and twist upon my bed.

Author's Note:
The December 2019 issue of *The Countryman* magazine reports on news from the Countryside Restoration Trust that barn-owl numbers in Cambridge are on the increase thanks to work carried out by that trust in its association with the leading barn-owl researcher and conservationist Colin Shawyer.

Storm clearing. Photograph by Stephen Russell Mendham.

KEEPING WITHIN THE LINES

When the universe exploded from the constraining shell of the cosmic egg, it ambitiously expanded to its current size, but unexpectedly found itself once again constrained, this time by the many forms of defining lines. Some lines are real and solid. Others are metaphorical. Yet others are invisible. Some lincs are restrictive, but others are helpful and useful.

"Let us take a walk then, you and I" was the invitation of that tepid lover, J. Alfred Prufrock, in the poem written by T. S. Eliot. Yes, let us take a walk and let us see what other kinds of lines there may be apart from lines of poetry.

All along the aerial messaging lines above our heads, resembling crotchets on a stave, the feathered throngs are gathering, summoning latecomers with twittering music. The swallows are preparing for their journey to a distant land.

All along the lines of furrowed soil offering warm, welcoming fast food behind the plough, shrieking crews of seagulls swarm in chaos, driven inland in search of easy pickings.

All along the parallel metal lines, like a caterpillar on a satin-bound ribbon, the jointed trains are carrying humans to their distant destinations; and competing cars follow their own lines, fulfilling the needs of the world's ever restless populations.

All along the lines of thought, universities, those hotbeds of unrest, create problems that would not otherwise exist. "There is nothing either good or bad, but thinking makes it so," said Hamlet.

All along the invisible criss-crossing ley lines harnessed by ancient man, who believed them to be a vibrant power source, ancient monuments such as Stonehenge and Avebury can be found, constrained and linked for ever.

All along lines of forbidding barbed wire we can find lands that separate the many tribes of people whose languages and customs differ, if our present walk takes us further abroad.

All along the horizontal lines of Cancer and Capricorn, the equator follows like a strengthening arm holding the pulsing globe together above its inner furnace and cauldron of boiling magma. But lines conjured up by human imagination cannot completely control the inner wrath of the earth, which will cascade and roar out through the volcanoes that are the planet's sores.

Having travelled so far, it would be best for us to stop and reflect. What would the world be like without lines? In former times, Romanies and other travellers would dry their washing by spreading it out on briars. Would we return to that practice in the absence of washing lines? What would happen to British Telecom if telephone lines disappeared? Would the world be a better place without the threatening lines of barbed wire that protect the lands claimed by previous entrepreneurs? How would commerce continue without shipping lines or airlines?

On the whole, there would seem to be a good argument for the universe to keep within the lines it fretted against when it expanded after exploding from the constraining shell of the cosmic egg. Or something along those lines.

Part Three

Verse and Worse

QUASIMODO'S SONG

The bells, the bells of Notre Dame
   Send startled pigeons wheeling.
    They punctuate the prayers
    Of those at altar kneeling.

This is my home; their clanging airs
   Sound just above my ceiling.
I watch with pride and count with care
The pilgrims summoned by their pealing.

When day is done, my home is bare,
   I see the shadows stealing.
   How glad I am that I can share
   My space of spiritual healing.

HE STOLE MY HEART

We met by chance.
He stole my heart.
I loved his soft green eyes.
He stole my heart.
I loved his thick blond hair.
He stole my heart.
His hand in mine was firm and strong.
He stole my heart.
He seemed at home when I asked him in.
He stole my heart.
And when he left . . .
He stole my wife.

BODYGUARD

Bodyguard, Bodyguard, say you'll be mine!
Say you'll protect me time after time!

Bodyguard, Bodyguard, twenty-four-seven
You are my choice from the county of Devon!

Bodyguard, Bodyguard, fear no rejection!
I've chosen you straight from a baffling selection!

Bodyguard, Bodyguard, be ready to act!
I'm a very busy woman, and that is a fact!

Bodyguard, Bodyguard, say you'll be mine!
Say you'll protect me time after time!
You're the best antiperspirant a busy girl could find!

IMPULSE AND CONSEQUENCE

This salmon's leap may be his last.
But yes, he has to do it.
The impulse comes from deep inside –
He knows he can't subdue it.

The praying mantis awaits his bride,
His impulse stronger than life.
How can he know on his honeymoon
He'll be a banquet for his wife?

The scent of cheese for Little Mouse
Brings messages of flavour.
Her impulse takes her inside the trap.
Alas! It's much too late to save her.

I've pondered all these warning tales,
But still I can't deny
The impulse in my watering mouth
To eat that huge mince pie!

Author's Note:
The salmon is born in fresh water. When it reaches about eight inches long, it swims from the river in which it is born into the sea, where it will spend up to five years. As a mature fish, it makes its way back to the river of its birth, sometimes encountering rapids and sometimes making spectacular leaps up waterfalls. The journey alone can exhaust this courageous creature. If the salmon survives the journey back to the place of its birth, it will mate, and the female will lay eggs. Both male and female salmon will then die, completely exhausted.

In some circles it is believed that the instinct to mate and procreate is stronger than the instinct to stay alive. In the case of the praying mantis, after mating the female will bite off the head of the male and then dine on the corpse!

MYSTIQUE

Mystique is my name, mystique my nature.
My tail is long, but short my stature.
My charm is misread; less mention of that!
I am a very cuddlesome cat.

I leave home at night – I have my own door.
What I do then no one is sure.
My purpose in life? No one can guess.
I have no remorse, I have to confess.

My purpose is murder. I go out to kill
Anything defenceless – I've honed my skill.
Small furry things I torture with pleasure.
No need to kill quickly, I kill them at leisure.

Just before dawn I'm home once more.
I must tidy up, then I'll open my door.
I clean blood from my whiskers, mud from my paws.
I must not leave tracks on those telltale floors.

I head upstairs to my vassal's bed.
She stirs very gently and strokes my head.
I nuzzle and purr; she expects to be kissed.
My night's work's a mystery – I haven't been missed!

HOW IS IT . . . ?
The words of a grateful woman, addressed to her very best friend

How is it, my dear, we have travelled so far
And assumed we never would part?
For fifty-six years we have followed our star
And been faithful right from the start.

How is it, my dear, you've stayed close by my side
As we've travelled through life's changing fashions?
For better for worse we've remained starry-eyed
And ignored other people's strange passions.

How is it, my dear, that although we've grown old
I find you as alluring as ever?
Despite on your face I see wrinkles and folds,
I'm desperate to keep you for ever.

How is it, my dear, after so many years
We two are still together?
With a bashful face, my handbag replied,
"I'm made of best-quality leather!"

JINGLES THE TROUBADOUR

I jingle and I jangle as I spangle on my way.
I have no roof above my head, and my clothes begin to fray.
My boots have seen their better days, and water jingles in.
The stones will jangle my tender toes, for the soles are far too thin.

I jingle and I jangle as I spangle on my way.
I hope you crowds will mingle when you hear my guitar play.
My songs will fall upon the air and birds will soon join in,
So follow me, forget your cares, and enjoy my merry din.

I jingle and I jangle as I spangle on my way.
The sun will always shine on me and brighten up my day.
The road I tread is calling me; the stars will give me light.
I'm Jingles, your troubadour, and I wish you all goodnight!

Author's Note:
The troubadour was a medieval musician and poet who roamed throughout Southern France, Northern Spain and Northern Italy, entertaining with his songs of chivalry and romance. The manuscripts of many of the songs written and performed by troubadours are still in existence today, including a record of the rules governing their form.